BY ALI BOVIS   ILLUSTRATED BY JEN TAYLOR

SYLVIE

Save the Beach

Calico

n Imprint of Magic Wagon
abdobooks.com

FOR JASON, MY EVERYTHING,
THANK YOU FOR EVERY DAY. —AB

FOR MARC AND MY FAMILY. —JT

abdobooks.com

Published by Magic Wagon, a division of ABDO,
PO Box 398166, Minneapolis, Minnesota 55439. Copyright
© 2020 by Abdo Consulting Group, Inc. International copyrights reserved
in all countries. No part of this book may be reproduced in any form
without written permission from the publisher. Calico™ is a trademark
and logo of Magic Wagon.

Printed in the United States of America, North Mankato, Minnesota.
092019
012020

THIS BOOK CONTAINS
RECYCLED MATERIALS

Written by Ali Bovis
Illustrated by Jen Taylor
Edited by Bridget O'Brien
Art Directed by Candice Keimig

Library of Congress Control Number: 2019942382

Publisher's Cataloging-in-Publication Data

Names: Bovis, Ali, author. | Taylor, Jen, illustrator.
Title: Save the beach / by Ali Bovis ; illustrated by Jen Taylor.
Description: Minneapolis, Minnesota : Magic Wagon, 2020. | Series: Sylvie; book 2
Summary: When faced with the possible closing of her favorite beach, Sylvie
    first attempts a one-person coastal cleanup march on city hall, but thanks to the town
    clown, she realizes it will take more than one person to save the beach.
Identifiers: ISBN 9781532136528 (lib. bdg.) | ISBN 9781644943205 (pbk.) | ISBN 9781532137129
    (ebook) | ISBN 9781532137426 (Read-to-Me ebook)
Subjects: LCSH: Beach closures--Juvenile fiction. | Beach cleanup--Juvenile fiction. |
    Ecology--Juvenile fiction. | Team work in fund raising--Juvenile fiction. | Self-assurance--
    Juvenile fiction. | Friendship--Juvenile fiction.
Classification: DDC [Fic]--dc23

TABLE OF CONTENTS

Chapter 1
Bake Sale at the Beach 4

Chapter 2
Save the Beach! 16

Chapter 3
March on City Hall 27

Chapter 4
Coastal Cleanup 39

Chapter 5
Mr. Twist 'n' Shout 53

Chapter 6
Everybody, Everywhere 65

Chapter 7
The Seagulls of Sea View 74

Chapter 8
The Big Day 82

Chapter 9
Get in Position 93

Chapter 10
Say "Beach!" 105

BAKE SALE AT THE BEACH

Sylvie shoved her sign in the sand and double-checked her watch. The hour hand ticked to the endangered black rhinoceros's nose.

Was it really almost nine? How did it get so late?

Sylvie thought about her Saturday morning. She'd eaten rainbow-sprinkle pancakes for breakfast, as usual. Then she had alphabetized her endangered animals trading cards. Watched reruns of the Earth Day concert on TV with her adopted puppy, Snickers. And helped her best friend, Sammy, give his turtle her eye drops.

Time flies when you're having fun. But she was *finally* at the beach. She needed to get this bake sale started!

Sylvie set up her table in the shade and took in the view. Her heart felt full.

Sea View Beach was truly the most special place in the world. The bright California sun glistened on the water. The white warm sand sparkled on the shore. A heap of trash tumbled down a dune.

Wait, what? Trash? On the beach? *Her* beach?!

Sylvie felt a jolt. She turned and noticed Sammy freeing a sand crab from an old shoe. She remembered it was just last week they found a sea turtle stuck in plastic. Not OK!

And what in the world had her little brother, Henry, found now? Other peoples' old food? Yuck!

Sylvie's parents brought over the last supplies from the car. Sylvie gave her head a shake and turned back to the table.

Focus, she told herself. Today was important. Sylvie would run her bake sale first. "Then I'll get to the bottom of this messy beach business!" she whispered.

She looped Snickers's leash around a table leg and flipped through her clipboard.

"Have fun!" said her mom, shifting the beach umbrella to her shoulder. "We'll be in our regular spot if you need anything."

"Bye!" Sylvie said. She stretched her arms behind her back and checked out the action on the beach.

Sammy was examining a critter

crawling in the rocks. Henry banged on the closed snack bar window. Why bother? He could buy a cookie from her in a few minutes.

Sylvie felt something bump her head. Something soft. Something fluffy. She turned to see a fuchsia puffball charm dangling on a camera strap.

"Doing your pre-bake-sale warm-ups?" asked her former friend, Camilla.

"Yep," said Sylvie, coming out of a lunge. "I'm ready to open."

Camilla strutted off. Sylvie shrugged. Who knew why Camilla didn't get in line for a cookie. Or what she was up to. Sylvie had more important things to worry about.

She flipped her sign to "open" and soon a crowd gathered. Sylvie pulled out a megaphone. "Thanks for your support," she said. She swatted a seagull away and turned the volume up.

"Last week's bake sale for new recycle bins at school was a big success." Sylvie skimmed her clipboard. Aww, the poor lemurs.

"This week I'm raising money for endangered lemurs. They are losing their rain forests. People are hunting them. We have to do something!"

Sammy spoke up. "Lemurs can jump more than thirty feet as they move from tree to tree."

"Stellar!" Sylvie said. "OK, everyone. Step right up."

As always, the beach had lots of great customers. Sea View Beach was the best bake sale location in town. And not bad for swimming and sandcastle building either.

Sylvie smiled. Sea View Beach really was the best. All of it! Although, as she remembered with a frown, it was looking a bit dirty. And it was a bit smelly too.

But then, Sylvie saw something that took her mind off the trash. She climbed on top of her chair and waved her arms. She didn't want her favorite teacher, Ms. Martin, and Ms. Martin's *very important* husband to miss her.

"Ms. Martin!" Sylvie yelled into her megaphone. "Over here!"

The couple walked over. Ms. Martin put money in the donation box. "Looks like another successful event," she said.

"Oh yes," Sylvie said proudly. She handed her teacher some cookies. "We had a big rush of customers. These are the last ones!"

"This beach is a great spot," said Mr. Martin. "Too bad about the news."

"News?" Sylvie asked. What news? Mr. Martin worked at city hall. He always had the inside scoop.

"There has been so much pollution. It's endangering marine life, animals, plants, and it's not good for humans either," Mr. Martin answered. "We're talking about it at city hall. It's not safe for people to be here. So we might need to—"

Sylvie panicked. "Might need to what?" she interrupted. "I've got to help! Sea View Beach is the most stellar place, ever."

But then Sylvie saw the flyer sticking out of Mr. Martin's bag. It said, "Next Saturday: Vote on Beach Closure."

Sylvie gasped. Was she too late?

SAVE THE BEACH!

Could they really close the beach? Sylvie opened her mouth but nothing came out.

Please don't close the beach, she thought, pacing. Mr. and Ms. Martin munched on their cookies and chatted.

She couldn't lose her best bake sale spot. She remembered her first sale.

The Save the Whales people had told her they'd never seen an event like it. Who said four year olds can't count money? Or stand for six straight hours? She would've done anything for those poor whales with the plastic bags and bottles in their stomachs.

She stopped pacing and gripped the edge of the table. She took a deep breath and tried again. "Could they really close the beach?" she asked Mr. Martin.

Mr. Martin looked at Ms. Martin. Sylvie's favorite teacher looked sad.

"I'm afraid so," Mr. Martin replied.

Sylvie collapsed onto her folding chair, her head in her hands. Images of her best memories at the beach flashed through her mind.

Her first time riding a wave. Her first time burying Henry in the sand. Her first interpretive dance performance depicting the destruction of the planet's natural resources.

Mr. Martin went on. "We need

to protect the animals, plants, and
marine life. The people of Sea View,
too. Unless there's a big change before

next weekend, I expect we will vote to close it."

Sylvie's head popped up. "Wait. Did you say 'big change'?" Everything came into focus again.

"That's right," Mr. Martin replied.

Sylvie pushed her visor up and straightened out. Big change? Big change was her middle name! Actually it was Adrian. But she wished it could be Big change.

Sylvie grabbed her clipboard. She flipped for blank paper and started a list: *Big Change to Save the Beach.*

She capped her pen. Sylvie crammed her things in a tote and grabbed the dog's leash. "Big change, coming up!"

Ms. Martin gave Sylvie a wink. "You can do it!"

Sylvie hurried off. Walking along the sand, she noticed the beach had filled up. So had the trash cans. She picked up her pace, hurrying to Sammy.

Sylvie poured water from a bottle into a portable dog bowl for Snickers. Then she gave Sammy the full update.

"I've got to save the beach! If it closes, I can't imagine the consequences. No more helping the whales. Or the lemurs. Or even the recycle bins."

Sammy hunched over a hermit crab. "Save the beach from what?" The crab retreated into his soda bottle cap.

"From closing," Sylvie replied. She poked the cap. "From trash like this. Hermit crabs belong in shells. Not bottle caps!"

Sylvie started scribbling across the back of the flyer and rattled off the details. "Too much pollution. City hall vote. Big Change. I'm working on an idea. I'm the only one who can save it."

She marched along the picnic area with Snickers, thinking and writing. Then she hurried back toward Sammy with a plan: a march on city hall.

Sammy gently drew the crab out of the soda bottle cap. "You're right," he said, guiding the crab into a shell. "We need to look out for everyone. I hope you can save the beach. So, you want help?" Sammy stood up tall.

Was Sammy offering to help? Then another crab crawled over, and Sylvie realized he must have been talking to the crabs about helping.

Of course, the animals could help! Why hadn't she thought of that sooner? Sylvie jotted another idea: an animal sit-in to save the beach.

"Thanks, Sammy. The animals will be a big help! They can protest the beach closing by sitting together and not budging. They'll send a message to protect their home."

Sammy tilted his head. He shrugged his shoulders and took a mouthful of fries.

Before long, Sylvie had scribbled ideas down the sheet. By the time she reached her parents' blanket, her list had grown.

Big Change to Save the Beach:

- March on city hall
- Animal "sit-in"
- Post signs to protect wildlife and prevent littering
- Bake cookies to make the beach smell good
- Spruce up the beach with sand sculptures
- Ask the mayor and city hall officials to protect the beach
- Bake sale to raise money to keep the beach clean
- Get more trash cans and recycle bins for the beach
- Spread the word
- Beach cleanup?

Sylvie had just finished reading the list to her parents when she heard a series of clicking sounds.

"You're working on a project too?" asked a familiar voice.

MARCH ON CITY HALL

The ever-present puffball charm hung from Sylvie's former best friend's camera. What did Camilla want now?

She had asked about the bake sale that morning. But she never bought a cookie. She'd just taken pictures and then walked away.

Pictures for what? Sylvie had no idea. And she could have sworn she heard Camilla whispering that the snickerdoodles had too many rainbow sprinkles. Too many rainbow sprinkles? As if that were even possible!

Camilla twirled the pin on her dress. "What are you up to now?"

Sylvie's face lit up. She had ten sparkly ideas for big change to save the beach. She was so excited, she'd even share the news with Camilla. "Well," she started.

"Sylvie!" Henry interrupted. "We're leaving!"

Sylvie looked up and noticed her mom was halfway up the dune headed to the parking lot.

Sylvie checked her watch. Both hands rested between the rhinoceros's horns. Ten o'clock! She was running out of time.

Sylvie scooped up her stuff. "Sorry, Camilla. I've gotta go! I'm marching on city hall!" Snickers tugged on his leash. "Right after I drop off Snickers. Oh, and grab my best marching sneakers."

"Your what?" asked Camilla.

She'd explain another time. Maybe. "Can't talk, bye!" she answered.

Sylvie's mom and Henry agreed to take her to city hall so she could put the first leg of her new plan into motion. Jumping out of the car, Sylvie leaned her megaphone and protest sign against a bus stop.

A soft breeze swept up the sun-drenched street. *Perfect weather for a march*, she thought.

Sylvie's mom walked toward the bookshop next door. "Are you sure you don't want our help?" she asked.

Henry skipped over. He stabbed a straw into his chocolate milk box. "Oops," he said. Brown liquid exploded everywhere.

Sylvie nodded. "I'm sure." She had to save the beach. There would be no time for little brothers or explosions of any kind. "I'll meet you after."

Sylvie looked at city hall. A woman with a briefcase walked by. She looked official.

Sylvie lifted her protest sign and turned the megaphone volume to the highest setting. "Save the beach!" she chanted while marching.

The woman kept walking.

Sylvie double-checked her volume. Two men crossed over.

She tried again. "Save the beach!"

No reaction. Sylvie double-checked her sign. Was something wrong with it? The purple writing popped. She'd included plenty of stars on her poster board.

Sylvie was second-guessing her choice in font color when a horde of people appeared from around the corner. They looked tall. And official. They all wore matching shirts.

They headed for her. Maybe they were high-level top secret officials. This was her chance. "SAVE THE BEACH!"

It worked! One of them headed straight toward her, smiling. Sylvie smiled back. The beach was as good as saved now. But then Sylvie noticed the lady's shirt had an emblem that said "West Coast Tours."

Sylvie's happy face faded. These were not super high-level top secret government officials. They were tourists.

Sylvie sighed. She helped the group with directions. Then she watched them walk off and said goodbye to any chance of her march succeeding.

How could she convince everyone to save the beach if no one was there to hear her? No city hall officials. No news cameras. Not even the hot-dog cart guy. Where could they all be?

Sylvie slumped onto a bench and felt her stomach growl. She put down her things and pulled out a granola bar. She took a bite then heard a rattling noise behind her.

A man wheeled a garbage container to the curb. "Sylvie?" he asked.

Sylvie turned around. It was Hank, director of sanitation. He had been

Sylvie's contact at city hall for her school recycling bin project. She left her snack and jumped up. "Hank!"

"What's happening?" he asked.

"There's going to be a vote to close the beach. I need to stop them," she answered. "But where is everyone?"

"Let me see." Hank scrolled through his phone.

Sylvie went back for her snack. The day's excitement had made her work up an appetite. But all that remained were a few lonely oats and a picked-apart wrapper.

She heard the swooshing of wings and saw something fly off from the corner of her eye. That pesky seagull. He must have followed her!

"Here they are," Hank said, pointing to a calendar. Sylvie could not wait to hear where the officials could be. The Governor's Mansion? The White House? The International Space Station?

COASTAL CLEANUP

Sylvie learned that the city hall officials were not at the International Space Station or any of the other spots she had imagined. It turned out they were a bit closer to home.

Sylvie swung open the door at Pinky Nails. She had never held a march in a nail salon before. But no matter! She readied her sign and megaphone. Then she looked around.

A Grand Opening banner hung. Two halves of a ribbon rested on the floor. An oversized scissors sat on the table.

No mayor. No deputy mayor. No other city hall officials. Just a bunch of people getting their nails painted and a lot of pink lemonade.

"Where is everyone?" she asked. Ms. Lee explained it had been a wonderful opening celebration, but the mayor and other VIP guests had gone home.

Sylvie needed to process the news. She set down her things and sank into an oversized massage chair. But only for a minute. She couldn't drink her pink lemonade with her hands full.

She lifted her feet as someone swept confetti away with a broom. A new idea started to form in Sylvie's head

And then, she was interrupted. *Click, click, click.*

Sylvie looked to see a flashing light. A familiar face. And a puffball charm dangling from a camera strap. Camilla tightened the cover on her camera lens. "What were you marching for?"

Only the most important thing ever, thought Sylvie. But what would Camilla care? She had just been taking pictures. Who knows what for—probably extra credit.

Then the sweeper circled back and Sylvie remembered her new plan. "Sorry. Gotta go," she said. "I'm off to save the beach."

She recycled her lemonade cup and grabbed her sign. Then she sprinted to the bookshop. "Mom, Henry!" Sylvie ran circles around them. "We need to get to the hardware store!"

"What's going on? Why is your face all pink?"

"I just had a few cups of lemonade," Sylvie puffed.

"I know how to save the beach. Can we please go to the hardware store? And then the beach? No one was around for my march. But if I can clean the beach, it will be safe for everyone. Then it will *have* to stay open."

Sylvie's mom smiled and brought her in for a squeeze. "Sounds like a great plan. Dad is probably still at the beach, so you can fill him in, too."

After a quick trip to the hardware store, Sylvie, Henry, and their mom were back at the beach. They walked to where Sylvie's dad was asleep on their blanket.

"Sweetie, we'd love to help clean." Her mom nudged her dad under the umbrella.

Sylvie appreciated the offer. But this was something she needed to do herself.

No one else could be trusted with such a task. What if other people put the garbage in the recycling bags? Or the recycling in the garbage bags?

The beach would never get cleaned properly. It would be closed down and she could never have another bake sale there to help any causes. The whales, the lemurs, the world! They were all counting on Sylvie Schwartz!

"Thanks, but I've got this." Sylvie tore into her supplies. She grabbed the trash picker and got to work, more determined than ever.

She started by putting a glass bottle in a recycling bag. Many more cropped up after that.

The bottles didn't just come in glass. She collected plastic bottles, along with plastic bottle caps, straws, and lids. And

so many old plastic bags, forks, spoons, and sporks, too.

Sylvie tackled paper next. As she strode along the beach, she shoved

newspapers, magazines, and wrappers
into recycling bags.

Then she moved to cans. Soda cans.
Fishing bait cans. Silly string cans.

As her hour hand ticked toward the black rhinoceros's bow tie, Sylvie moved faster. She sprinted across the beach and collected all kinds of trash.

Sylvie tied the bags tight. "Perfect."

She inspected the beach and discovered one last problem. Oh no! That sand wouldn't do. It was filthy and lumpy, too! But how could she clean it with everyone there?

Sylvie pulled out her megaphone. "Wake up, people. Grab your blankets, towels, and umbrellas. Please move to the parking lot."

Slowly, most people made their way off the beach. *Why was everyone grumbling?* Sylvie wondered.

When the sand needed to be raked, the sand needed to be raked. She would be finished in no time. How long could it take to rake the sand, polish the rocks, and shine the seaweed anyway?

By the end of the day, the beach was so clean, it actually sparkled. "Stellar!"

Sylvie nudged a seagull trying to break into her trash bags. Was that a piece of granola stuck in his feathers? Hadn't he eaten enough already?

"Shoo!" She watched him fly off. Soon, Sylvie's family crowded around.

"Amazing job," said her dad.

"We're proud of you," said her mom.

Sylvie's parents weren't the only ones thankful. The entire crowd seemed to be cheering.

"It's about time you finished!" said a man, laying out his blanket.

"Really!" hollered a woman.

Sylvie smiled. It felt great to hear such praise. She couldn't wait to get home and tell Snickers and Sammy. Plus they won't believe the town was considering closing the beach. It only took her half a day to clean it.

As Sylvie got in the car, a yawn escaped. She had worked hard. But it was worth it. The beach was clean and she, Sylvie Schwartz, had saved it!

Orange and pink wisps cropped up in the sky as the Schwartzes backed out of the lot. Sylvie rolled down her window for a better view. And then she noticed something—the faint smell of baby food.

As her dad drove away, Sylvie twisted in her seat. She was trying to figure out why the beach would smell like mushed bananas. Her dad kept driving. She gave up and leaned back.

Oh well. It was probably nothing.

MR. TWIST 'N' SHOUT

Sylvie spooned sprinkles over her eggs and took a bite of pancake.

Snickers barked and sprinted to the door. A second later, Sylvie heard four knocks. Three loud and one soft. Sammy's knock.

"Sammy?" Sylvie hadn't been expecting him. But she couldn't wait to share the amazing news about the beach.

She opened the door to find Sammy, holding a box. She peeked inside. "Hi, Shelly."

"Can you help?" Sammy asked. "She won't come out of her shell for her medicine. Mom and Dad tried too. Nothing is working."

Poor turtle. Those eye drops probably stung. "Sure," she replied. "I have all day. I already cleaned the entire beach. It's so stellar. They'll never close it now."

"That's awesome!" said Sammy.

"What do you think will get her out?" she asked. "I have a new snickerdoodle scented candle. Maybe she'd like to smell it? Or I can read to her from *Kid Activist Monthly*. Snickers and I are in the middle of an incredible article."

"Hmm. Those are great ideas," he said. "But maybe can you try holding these pieces of carrots and lettuce?"

Sylvie thought about it. "Sure. That might work too. Come on in. Be back in a minute. I'm going to grab the paper."

Sylvie skipped to the mailbox. "Seriously?" she asked the seagull, perched on top. "There's not even food in there. Shoo!"

As the seagull took flight, Sylvie heard a familiar sound. *Click, click, click.*

She turned and spied Camilla crouched behind the bushes. Would Camilla just knock it off with all her picture taking already?

Sylvie sighed. No matter. She opened the mailbox and pulled out the thick newspaper. Maybe there'd be an article about how she saved the beach!

But when she looked down, the most terrible headlines leapt off the page.

"Vote to Close Polluted Beach: Next Saturday"

"Beloved Children's Performer Rocks Sea View Again: Toddlers Twist & Shout For More"

"No! OH NO!" She ran inside. Sammy was waiting for her in the kitchen. Sylvie flopped onto a chair.

"Are you OK?" he asked. "What happened?"

Only the worst thing imaginable! she thought. Toddlers Night Out destroyed the beach. Not even Sylvie could clean it. The trash, the recycling, the juice boxes!

Sammy lifted Shelly out of her box. He walked to Sylvie's chair. "Sylvie?"

She just shook her head. "So many juice boxes," was all she could get out. "And all those straws!"

"Huh?"

Sylvie took a deep breath. Then she handed Sammy the newspaper. "The beach. It's ruined. Again. All my work, for nothing. Now they will have to close it."

SEA VIEW TIMES

BELOVED CHILDREN'S PERFORMER ROCKS SEA VIEW AGAIN: TODDLERS TWIST & SHOUT FOR MORE

VOTE TO CLOSE POLLUTED BEACH NEXT SATURDAY

She blinked back tears. Those poor whales with all that plastic in their bellies. The innocent turtles and crabs trapped in litter on the shore. What if one was Shelly's cousin?

Sammy got a worried expression on his face. "What about the animals and marine life?" He put down the newspaper and hugged Shelly.

"I know," Sylvie sighed. The rainbow sprinkles tube caught her eye. "And what about my bake sales? I'll never find a spot as perfect as the beach. Mr. Twist 'n' Shout ruined everything!"

Sammy was quiet for a minute. "And to think, we used to like that guy," he mumbled.

Sylvie scanned the kitchen counter. The old CD was still in a pile under the stereo.

Mr. Twist 'n' Shout, what have you done? she thought, picking it up. Mr. Twist 'n' Shout winked from under a tricolored wig. She flipped over the CD case and skimmed the songs.

Sammy scratched Shelly's head. "Maybe we can think of another idea for the beach?"

Sylvie tapped her fingers. Could they come up with another idea in time?

"What about your Big Change list?" asked Sammy. "And I can help too."

Sylvie's list of ideas for Big Change. Of course! "Sammy, you're a genius!"

Sylvie had been so focused on the cleanup, she had forgotten her other ideas. And as she watched Sammy pat his turtle's shell, she realized it would be great to have his help, too. Maybe she couldn't do this alone after all.

Sylvie was so happy she felt like celebrating. She looked down. Mr. Twist 'n' Shout stared at her, all festive in his polka-dotted striped jumpsuit.

Before she could stop herself, she put the CD in the stereo and pressed the green arrow. "Just one last time," she whispered.

Sylvie heard the sound of the songs shuffling. Then the shuffling stopped. And the strangest thing happened. Song seven. Sylvie had heard it so many times before.

But today, it took on a new meaning. She picked up the CD case and stared at the words inside: "Clean up. Clean up. Everybody. Everywhere. Clean up. Clean up. Everybody do your share."

As the rainbow-colored crooner's voice filled the room, his words gave Sylvie yet another idea for Big Change. A new way to save the beach. Her beach. And this time, save it for good!

But first, she needed to help a turtle with an eye infection. Sylvie grabbed her magazine and candle.

EVERYBODY, EVERYWHERE

Principal Close sounded surprised to hear from Sylvie Sunday night. Was ten o'clock too late for Sylvie to call? But beach cleanup waits for no one, Sylvie figured.

On Monday morning, Sylvie reported to the principal's office first thing. Ms. Martin came along too.

Principal Close agreed to let Sylvie make a morning announcement. All she had to do in return was never call Principal Close at home again.

Sylvie leaned into the microphone. "Testing. One, two, three. Is this on?"

Principal Close nodded.

Sylvie pushed a button until a screechy sound blasted through the office. "Can it get louder?"

Principal Close jumped. She covered her ears and shook her head. Ms. Martin smiled funny. She covered the microphone and lowered the volume. "You're all set," she said.

Sylvie took one last glance at her

announcement. "Listen up, people. You may have read this in the paper or watched it on the news. You may have heard my megaphone last night. Or caught sight of the flyers I put on every car, bicycle, and surfboard this morning."

Principal Close's eyes popped wider than an endangered spotted owl's. She was clearly very impressed by Sylvie's efforts.

Sylvie went on. "There's going to be a vote next Saturday to close Sea View Beach. It's too polluted. It's a danger to animals, marine life, plants, and people, too. It's a danger to our entire ecosystem and the world itself!"

Principal Close pointed at the clock. Sylvie needed to finish. "I tried to fix the problem myself. It did not work. Which was surprising considering how many other things I've been able to fix.

"Anyway, to save the beach," she said, taking a breath. "It's going to take everybody, everywhere."

Principal Close scooped up the microphone. "Thank you, Sylvie." She rubbed inside her ear and lowered the volume. "Anyone interested in helping can visit Ms. Martin's classroom after school."

Sylvie leaned over and blurted into the microphone. "That's right, today and every day this week! Come all!"

"Whoops!" Sylvie said as her hand knocked into Principal Close's mug.

Who knew such a tiny bit of tea could cover an entire desk. Hopefully the soaked stack of "State Tests" wasn't too important. She turned to Principal Close.

"Sorry," she mouthed as she left.

When the classroom clock ticked to 2:59, Sylvie cleared her desk.

Buzz! School was finally out. Time to plan for the Big Change.

Sylvie pulled out a megaphone from her cubby. Kids from other classes filed in. Sylvie raced to greet them.

Ms. Martin wedged a stopper in the door. People from all around town

showed up. Sylvie had never seen the classroom so crowded. Not one inch of the solar system rug was visible. Not even a star. The room became warm.

Ms. Martin opened a window and then nodded to Sylvie.

Sylvie gave a thumbs-up and looked around as she spoke.

"Thanks for volunteering to save the beach. I've divided tasks into groups. From organizing an animal sit-in, to sprucing up the beach with sand sculptures, each group has different projects. Please sign up for one."

Sylvie's friend Josh raised a hand. "I'm in!" he said.

"Me too!" said Josh's twin brother, Nick.

A smile spread across Sylvie's face. Her plan was working. First Josh and Nick, soon the whole town would want to help!

Before long, everyone had signed up. Everyone, Sylvie suddenly realized, except Camilla.

THE SEAGULLS OF SEA VIEW

Classic, thought Sylvie. Camilla was probably still mad about the puffball. Or possibly about how Sylvie's puppy ate her entire lunch last Saturday. But anyway, where was she?

Click, click, click.

White feathers popped out of Sylvie's cubby. A seagull in the classroom? A familiar puffball ponytail rubber band bobbed nearby.

There stood Camilla, snapping pictures as usual. How did that seagull get inside?

Then Sylvie remembered Ms. Martin opening the window because the room had become so hot with all the people. But really, *what* was Camilla doing taking pictures of him?

Sylvie reached under her desk and pulled out one last poster. "There is one more group. It may be the most important group yet."

Sylvie glanced at her former best friend. With everyone else signed up already, Sylvie needed Camilla now more than ever. If she would just put down that camera.

"What is it for?" asked Camilla.

"Just the biggest-ever beach bake sale." Sylvie took a breath before asking Camilla something she'd not asked her in a long time. "Can you help?"

Camilla looked like she was thinking hard. Then Sylvie saw a small smile spread from the corner of Camilla's mouth. "Well," she started.

Sylvie waited excitedly. Was Camilla going to help?

Just then, more sounds echoed down the hall. Bells. Whistles. Maracas?

Orange, green, and purple spaghetti-hair appeared in the doorway.

Swish! Swish! Swish!

All of a sudden, the maracas stopped. The bells and whistles too. Confetti fell to the floor. Cheers erupted from the imagination station and the book nook.

The seagull pumped its wings across the room. He landed in the orange, green, and purple spaghetti-hair nest.

Wow, Sylvie thought. Mr. Twist 'n' Shout, here, in her own classroom!

Click, click, click.

And to make matters worse, Camilla was taking pictures of the chaos.

Sylvie spun around. What in the world? "Seriously, people. With all the excitement, you'd think the mayor herself was here!"

Sylvie huffed. "What are *you* doing here, Twist 'n' Shout? I had the beach all clean. It's your fault it got dirty again."

Click, click, click.

Sylvie shot a look at her former best friend. "And Camilla, enough already. What is with these pictures?"

"Actually," Camilla started.

"Sorry about the beach," Mr. Twist 'n' Shout cut in. He handed Sylvie a tissue-paper carnation. "I'm here to help."

Sylvie considered it. All those juice boxes. But he wanted to help. And this was the guy who wrote "It's Raining Sprinkles." He couldn't be all bad. "I guess we do need everyone," she said.

"I'll help too," Camilla added. "As I was trying to say, I've got all the pictures I need anyway."

Sylvie perked up. "What are those pictures for?" she finally asked.

"I'm in a photography class at the camera shop," Camilla replied. "My subject is the seagulls of Sea View."

Mr. Twist 'n' Shout tightened his red rubber nose. He pointed to the bird perched on his head and struck a pose. "Ooh, everyone loves the Sea View seagulls. Here. Take a picture of us!"

Huh, thought Sylvie. Then a glimmer of an idea sparked in her head.

THE BIG DAY

Sylvie leapt out of bed and got dressed. After all that planning, the big day was finally here.

Sylvie ran to her parents' room. "Let's go!" She banged on Henry's door. "We've got a beach to save."

Outside, stars still twinkled. Owls hooted. Six o'clock in the morning might seem early to go to the beach. But not for Sylvie. Not today!

The Schwartzes' car pulled into the lot as the sun came up over the Pacific. Sylvie led Henry and Snickers in stretches and then set up. Before long, Sammy arrived, then Camilla. Eventually the whole lot was full.

Sylvie pulled a pacifier off a baby crab's claw. "Poor little guy!" she said, passing Snickers's leash to Henry.

They needed to get to work. She climbed on top of her chair. She looked out into the sea of people armed with gloves, bags, garbage pinchers, and rakes. Everyone had come together.

TRASH BAGS

84

Everyone wanted to help. She felt a little catch in her throat. "Welcome, people. You know what to do. Let's save our beach!"

Sammy broke off with his group. They headed to the animal sit-in area.

Of all the animals, Snickers was the first to participate. He was doing such a fantastic job sitting. He had even fallen asleep!

After the sit-in, Sammy's group grabbed their signs and walked around. They knew not to disrupt the beach wildlife. They tiptoed and carefully staked "Turtle Nesting" and "No Littering" signs in the sand.

"Stellar!" Sylvie said.

Next, Sylvie checked Henry's group's work. Cinnamon swirled in the air. Fresh-baked cookies should always be the first step of any beautification effort. Sand sculptures too.

Thump! Sylvie looked up. Mr. Martin dropped a broken, old oar into a massive trash pile. Ms. Martin layered a beat-up boogie board on top.

The Martins weren't the only ones cleaning. A whole group of grown-ups was at work. Sylvie's dad collected trash. Her mom gathered recyclables. And, to Sylvie's surprise, Mr. Twist 'n' Shout was outpacing them all.

The grown-ups piled their bags onto the mountains of trash and recycling Sylvie's friends had already started.

But what was taking the city hall officials so long to get to the beach? Reporters might be there soon to film for the nightly news. Everything had to be perfect.

Sylvie reached for her rake, but something got it first. Something white. Something feathery. *Squawk!*

Sylvie looked the seagull in the eyes. "Don't even think about it!"

The seagull took off as Ms. Martin called Sylvie's name. Ms. Martin was pointing too. Sylvie followed her teacher's finger to the mayor and the other city hall officials. They came!

Sylvie's heart raced. She practiced her speech and ran to greet them.

"Thank you for coming!" she said.

After that, Sylvie hoped she remembered to say something about how the town had come together for the cleanup. And how they would never make such a mess that could potentially harm the animals, marine life, plants, and their fellow citizens again.

So could they keep the beach open? And what was the mayor's favorite flavor of ice cream?

In reality, it was all a blur. The last thing Sylvie remembered was thanking them for coming.

Then the mayor smiled and started to talk. Sylvie was so nervous and excited that she couldn't concentrate. Finally, the mayor patted Sylvie on the shoulder and walked away.

Sammy and Camilla ran over.

"How did it go?" asked Sammy.

Sylvie grinned but didn't answer.

Camilla waved her hand in front of Sylvie's face. "Well?"

Applause erupted from the lifeguard stand. Sylvie turned and saw her dad near the mayor. He signaled with a thumbs-up.

"Good . . . I think," she managed to get out. Fragments of their conversation came back to her. "Amazing work. Recommend we keep it open. Mint chocolate-chip or strawberry swirl."

Camilla looked at Sammy. "What is she talking about?"

Sammy turned to Sylvie. "Ah, Sylvie?"

Then Sylvie noticed the bake sale tables. She needed to focus.

"Yes, it was all good. But remember, even if the beach can stay open, we still need to make sure everyone keeps it clean. To the tables!"

Soon, Sylvie and Camilla were putting the finishing touches on the bake sale.

Everyone lined up. Sylvie powered on her megaphone. "Welcome to the biggest beach bake sale ever. All money raised will go to keeping the beach clean. Step right up."

The line went past the parking lot and all the way to Tents & Tents on Beach Street! It was hard to hear anything. Just shouts for cookies and cakes. And then, the faint flutter of wings.

GET IN POSITION

"No!" Sylvie shouted. "Shoo!"

Those birds could *not* get the bake sale food! They would make a mess and ruin everything. She could picture the newspaper headline now: "Coastal Cleanup Catastrophe!"

The seagulls advanced.

Snickers barked and lunged toward the sky.

Sylvie's heart raced.

Remember the plan, she told herself. Thank goodness she'd used her lunch break to strategize with her friends.

They had made a list of backup plans for any problem—rain, ants, and even seagulls. Though she had never imagined *this* many seagulls.

She turned her megaphone low and spoke calmly: "Table one. Table two. Table three. Table four. Get in position."

No response.

Seriously? "C'mon people!" she said louder. Nothing. She turned the volume all the way up. "POSITIONS!"

Her team jumped. Sylvie patted her megaphone as Sammy pulled out rolls of biodegradable wax paper. He tossed them to everyone. Working triple time, they pulled, stretched, and sealed. Soon everything was covered.

Still, the seagulls closed in. Gasps came from the crowd. Shrieks. The mayor covered her eyes.

Thump!

The first seagull landed.

Thump! Thump! Thump!

Sylvie looked at Mr. Twist 'n' Shout. He must have been thinking the same thing. Forget sprinkles. The sky was raining seagulls!

Thump! Thump! Thump!

Sylvie took a deep breath. Would the paper hold?

Squawk! A seagull punched through the paper at the cookie table. A small hole formed. He wiggled his beak. The hole became bigger. And bigger. Until finally, it was exactly rainbow sprinkled snickerdoodle size.

Squawk! Just like that, the seagull took off, cookie in beak.

Sylvie's biggest bake sale was ruined. How could she raise money to keep the beach clean? What about the poor whales, turtles, and everyone else?

What if the beach got dirty again? Would they have to live in pollution forever? What about her other projects to help Sea View and the world? Not to mention, no more swimming or sandcastle building.

She couldn't believe it. Once again, her plan had failed.

Sylvie blinked back tears. She looked at Camilla in a blur of feathers and cakes. Her old friend had thrown herself over the cake table, but it was no use.

The seagulls pecked at Camilla's puffball charm. They eventually took off with a slice of gluten-free double chocolate cake.

After Camilla had taken all those pictures, you would have thought the seagulls might have been nicer to her. Then Sylvie remembered Mr. Twist 'n' Shout and the seagulls at school.

"The pictures!" she said.

Sylvie ducked, weaved, and crawled to her supplies. "Sammy! Camilla!"

Sammy scaled the table. Camilla scrunched down in the sand. They made their way over.

The squawking got louder.

"Guys! I have a plan," Sylvie yelled.

"What is it?" hollered Camilla.

"How are we going to raise money to keep the beach clean?" yelled Sammy.

Sylvie gestured to her friends. They moved to a quieter spot.

"How are we going to raise money?" asked Sylvie. She pointed to the camera around Camilla's neck. "That's how!"

"Huh?" asked Sammy.

"Huh?" asked Camilla.

Sylvie looked at Mr. Twist 'n' Shout flung across the pie table. He really had tried to do his part.

"Remember everybody, everywhere? Let's include everybody, everywhere!" She pointed at a seagull.

Wait, what? Sylvie wondered.

This one was trying to eat something from the sea. But it was stuck on a stray piece of trash. That must have been hard. The poor seagulls. They must have just been hungry!

"It's their beach too!" she said.

Sylvie shared her new plan. She called Henry over and filled him in too. He helped update the bake sale signs.

Just in time! A second and third fleet of birds dive-bombed the tables. All the seagulls in the entire country must have flocked there.

"Ready?" asked Sylvie.

Sammy hurried to the tables and shoved the new signs in the sand. "Ready!"

Camilla turned on her camera. She positioned herself with a head-on shot of the tables. "Ready!"

Sylvie turned her megaphone to full blast. "Hello!"

No response. The screams, shrieks, and squawks continued.

Oh no! Sylvie didn't have enough sound power, even with the megaphone on high. No one could hear her over the sound of the seagulls.

Mr. Twist 'n' Shout must've noticed the same thing. He hurried over, his hand deep in that funny-looking bag he always carried.

He pulled out a horn and honked it. Then, he launched rainbow sprinkles from a confetti cannon. Finally, he lugged out a tall stool.

"Citizens of Sea View," he yelled into a microphone. "Sylvie Schwartz." He motioned to Sylvie.

Sylvie climbed up on the stool and took the microphone.

Seagulls swarmed.

SAY "BEACH!"

"Thanks for coming together for the beach," said Sylvie. "It seems we haven't included *everybody* in our effort. So, I present the seagulls of Sea View."

She pointed at the birds around the bake sale table and went on.

"The line starts at the cookie table. For this special event, you can have your picture taken with the world-famous Sea View seagulls. Money goes to protecting the beach and keeping it clean."

Soon, the photo line snaked up the dunes, past the parking lot, around Tents & Tents, through Sea View Laser Tag. It even went into the ice cream aisle of the gas station food mart.

At first some customers were put off by the seagulls. But Sylvie explained.

It had been hard for them to find proper food because of the trash. The seagulls were just hungry. Once the beach was cleaned, they could go back to eating from the shore again.

Sylvie would make certain they'd find fish and worms. Not plastic and cans.

In no time, everyone understood. And everyone wanted a picture. Even Mayor Flores, Mr. Martin, and the other city hall officials.

Many hours later, the entire town had participated. The donation jars overflowed. Camilla had started to complain of finger cramps from the hours of photo snapping.

A seagull landed on Sylvie's clipboard. Then a rainbow sprinkle fell from its beak.

"Nice work today," she said to the seagull. "I couldn't have done it without you!" It almost seemed that the bird smiled.

Ms. Martin cleared her throat. "Sylvie, why don't you get in a picture?"

Sylvie nodded and grabbed her team.

"Say 'beach!'" said Ms. Martin.

"Stellar!" said Sylvie.

Mr. Twist 'n' Shout packed his things. "Fantastic job."

Sylvie looked at his orange, purple, and green spaghetti-hair and giggled. "You too."

He started to walk away. Sylvie remembered the confetti cannon. "And don't forget to clean up the confetti," she yelled.